JACK
Lights, Camera, Action!

by Dawn Bentley   Illustrated by Cathy Diefendorf

This book is dedicated to my son, Jackson Bentley Harshbarger—an amazing little guy who has put a permanent smile on my face. With all my love, Mom — D.B.

To Emma — C.D.

Book copyright © 2005 Trudy Corporation

Published by Soundprints Division of Trudy Corporation, Norwalk, Connecticut.

Book design: Marcin D. Pilchowski
Book layout: Bettina M. Wilhelm

First Edition 2005
10 9 8 7 6 5 4 3 2 1
Printed in China

Acknowledgements:
    Soundprints would like to thank the staff at the American Veterinary Medical Association and its member veterinarians who assisted in reviewing the story and illustrations.

JACK
Lights, Camera, Action!

by Dawn Bentley   Illustrated by Cathy Diefendorf

4

As the sun peeks through the window, a Jack Russell terrier named Jack wakes up. After a few stretches and yawns, Jack races down the hall and into Sophie's bedroom. He barks until she wakes up.

"Good morning, Jack," says Sophie. "Let's get something to eat, and then we'll go to work."

Jack is one of the famous stars on the very popular television show *It's a Ruff Life.*

After breakfast, Sophie grabs a bag filled with the things she and Jack will need—a script, a grooming brush, and, of course, some special doggy treats. She puts on Jack's leash and they walk to the television studio.

When they arrive at the studio gate, the security guard waves to Jack.

6

Star Studios

As Jack and Sophie hurry across the studio lot to Stage 26, they see many interesting things along the way.

"Hey Jack!" waves an actor dressed in a spacesuit.

"Jack! You look *sooo* handsome today," says a glamorous movie star.

"Jack! Sophie!" waves the Assistant Director. "Glad you made it on time. Hop on the golf cart and I'll give you a ride to the set."

Jack and Sophie hurry inside the lit-up set. The director is ready to start filming.

"Where's Jack?" he asks. "We can't shoot the scene without him!"

"Ruff! Ruff!" barks Jack when he hears his name.

"There you are! Good to see you fella! Are you ready?"

Jack takes his position under the bright lights. Sophie is standing off to the side. Jack knows to pay close attention to Sophie's cues. Sophie will let him know if he is doing a good job.

As the director yells "ACTION!" the set comes to life. Sophie raises her hand, signaling Jack to sit on the couch.

"Jack!" says the mom character. "You know you're not supposed to be on the furniture."

Sophie lowers her hand and Jack springs from the couch.

"Jack!" says Billy, the son character. "You knocked over my game!"

14

15

"Cut!" yells the director. "Great work, everyone—
especially you, Jack. Now let's set up for the next scene."

Jack runs over to Sophie, who pats him on the head
and gives him a treat. "Good job, Jack."

16

The actors and Jack shoot two more scenes and then break for lunch. Everyone lines up at a long table filled with every kind of food imaginable. But none of this food is what Jack should be eating.

"I have your meal in the dressing room," says Sophie.

After Jack eats his lunch, he and Sophie take a walk. They love exploring the studio. Sometimes they see famous movie stars, sometimes they watch other shows being filmed, and sometimes an adoring fan recognizes Jack.

"Look, Mom! It's Jack!" says a young boy. "Can I have his autograph?" asks the boy.

"Dogs can't write," says his mom.

"Ah, but Jack is a very special dog," says Sophie. "Watch this."

Sophie pulls a special inkpad that is safe for Jack from her pocket and places it on the ground. Jack knows exactly what to do. First he puts a paw on the inkpad, and then he presses it on a piece of paper.

"Here's Jack's autograph," says Sophie.

After wiping Jack's paw, Sophie takes him back to the dressing room so they can rehearse the next scene.

In the next scene Jack has to make a big mess. If he does not do it right the first time, he'll have to get cleaned up and do it again.

Jack and Sophie practice thoroughly, which makes Jack tired. He stretches out in his favorite position to rest.

As Jack dozes, he hears a knock on the door. It's time for his next scene!

Lights are shining brightly on a set that looks like a kitchen. When the director yells "ACTION," Jack runs around, jumps up on the counter, steps on a cake, and spills a bag of flour. What a mess!

"CUT!" yells the director. "Jack, that was perfect!"

"Good boy," says Sophie, as she gives Jack a treat. Jack is a well-behaved dog. Misbehaving is only part of his performance.

After a hard day's work, Jack and Sophie relax in the park. Jack loves being a working dog, but most of all Jack loves being with Sophie!

28

Pet Health and Safety Tips

• Just as Jack learned the difference between good and bad behavior, all dogs need to be trained to behave correctly at home and in public. Your veterinarian may be able to help you find a good training program for your dog.

• Socialization with other adults, children and dogs is important for your pet's good conduct. Exposing a puppy to a variety of environments will help him feel comfortable in many different situations.

• Active dogs need an acceptable way to release energy so they stay out of mischief. Consider scheduling playtime with other dogs or participating in agility training. Ask your veterinarian to give your dog a wellness exam before beginning any new, vigorous activity.

• In 2003, the AKC changed the name of Jack Russell terriers to Parson Russell terriers. This more closely associates the name with the historical terrier originally bred by the Reverend John Russell in England

GLOSSARY

Studio: A place where movies, videos or other recordings are made.

Cue: Body movement, music or words that signal a person or animal to perform.

Scene: A single situation in a play or movie.

A Real-Life Pet Tale

Boone Narr owns an internationally renowned animal training facility in California. One of the dogs his staff has trained is Twister, a ten-year-old female terrier mix. Twister has a resume most actresses would envy! She has appeared in several movies and television shows, including *Pirates of the Caribbean* and *Mad About You*. She has also worked on many television commercials.

Twister's fame has not gone to her head—she wags her tail when greeted and enjoys playing with other dogs in the park.